Victoria House

Victoria House

Written by
JANICE SHEFELMAN

Illustrated by
TOM SHEFELMAN

GULLIVER BOOKS
HARCOURT BRACE JOVANOVICH
San Diego   Austin   Orlando

HBJ

Text copyright © 1988 by Janice Shefelman
Illustrations copyright © 1988 by Tom Shefelman

Library of Congress Cataloging-in-Publication Data
Shefelman, Janice Jordan, 1930-
Victoria house.
"Gulliver books."
Summary: An old Victorian house is moved from the
country to its new location on a city street, where a
family fixes it up and moves in.
[1. Dwellings—Fictions. 2. Moving of buildings,
bridges, etc.—Fiction] I. Shefelman, Tom, ill.
II. Title.
PZ7.S54115Vi 1988   [E]   86-33565
ISBN 0-15-200630-3
First edition
A   B   C   D   E

The illustrations in this book were done in ink line and watercolor
on D'Arches of France watercolor paper.
The display type was set in Bookman Meola
by Thompson Type, San Diego, California.
The text type was set in Adroit Light
by Central Graphics, San Diego, California.
Printed and bound by Tien Wah Press, Singapore
Production supervision by Warren Wallerstein and Eileen McGlone
Designed by Dalia Hartman

To our children
Karl and Daniel
who looked and listened while we read

Victoria House was vacant. The fields about her were grown
up in weeds, and no longer did cows graze in the side pasture.

Long ago, when Victoria was lived in and loved, her family would sit in the gazebo on summer evenings after their work was done and talk as dusk settled over the rolling hills. Children chased fireflies or played tag in the yard.

But now they were all gone. Only Victoria was left.

Down by the highway a big sign read *360 ACRES FOR SALE,* and tacked over it a smaller one said *SOLD*. Across the highway was an auto park where trucks brought dead cars with dented fenders and smashed windows. They were stacked one on top of the other and lay rusting where another farmhouse once stood.

One day a black and silver van turned onto Victoria's road. A man and woman got out.

"We're going to have to get rid of that old house," said the man. "I can see a boulevard lined with Spanish-style buildings running right through here. How does that sound, Sarah? You're the architect."

But Sarah could not take her eyes off the old house. Without a word she walked up the weedy path to the porch. After a moment, she climbed the steps and sat down in the gazebo. "Yes," she murmured, nodding her head.

"Sarah, what are you up to?"

"It's perfect," she called back. "Do you think this house could be moved all the way to the city?"

He chuckled. "If that's what you're set on, I wouldn't bet against it."

As they walked through the tall grass toward the river, Sarah looked back at Victoria standing at the top of the rise. "I'll be back," she said to the house.

A few days later Sarah returned with a man and a boy.

"What do you think?" she asked her husband.

"She does have possibilities," said Jess, smoothing his mustache thoughtfully.

"Can I explore?" asked the boy.

"Yes, Mason, but be careful."

Mason opened the front door slowly and peered inside. It was quiet, as though the house were waiting. The floor creaked when he stepped into the entry hall. Light from a window above the stairs shone on peeling wallpaper and draped cobwebs.

Sarah and Jess came to the doorway and
stood for a moment.

"Oh, Jess, look at the woodwork."

"Hmmm, beautiful dust collectors," he said,
his eyes glinting with mischief.

They walked from room to room and then up
the staircase to the second floor. Mason darted
back and forth, looking out windows,
opening doors, urging them to come see the
funny-looking bathroom.

Finally they climbed the narrow stairs to the attic.
"Can this be my room?" asked Mason.

Sarah and Jess looked at each other. Jess's mustache curled
up as he grinned.
"Yes," they said together.

Two days later Sarah returned with Big Earl, the house mover. They walked around Victoria studying the foundation.

"Can we move her, Earl?"

"Sure, but we'll have to cut her in two to go under the power lines," he said and spit on the ground.

For several weeks the movers worked getting Victoria ready. Sarah came to watch and to take measurements for her drawings.

Big Earl directed his four sons as they put steel beams under Victoria's first and second floors. Then they sawed her studs in two all around.

Finally the boys backed their rumbling trucks up to each corner of the house and attached tail chains to the long girders, front and rear.

"Okay, lift her up," Big Earl called, pointing up with his thumb.

When it was hoisted, wheels were rolled under Victoria's first floor, and Big Earl's truck pulled it out from under the upper story.

It was late afternoon by the time they got both floors on wheels and headed home for supper.

Big Earl and his boys returned at midnight. Sarah, Jess, and Mason came, too. When two police cars arrived, the parade was ready to begin.

Victoria filled the road from side to side and even hung over the edges. In front and behind, the police cars flashed their lights.

Up and down hills, around curves, the lumbering procession moved toward the distant lights of the city. Mason looked back at Victoria winding slowly along the road. She rumbled and creaked through the stillness of the night.

"Do you think anyone else in the world is doing this right now?" Mason asked.

"Only if they are crazy," Jess said, reaching back to tousle his son's hair.

"Only if they love a house," Sarah said quietly.

At the outskirts of the city, mirrored buildings reflected the parade as it passed under bright street lights. They rumbled along empty streets deeper and deeper into the city. Traffic signals flashed yellow and red.

Turning the corner at a small grocery store, they moved down Park Street. On one side was a triangular park and on the other a row of houses with well-tended gardens. Down the street was a library.

The trucks slowed and stopped. There, on an empty corner lot,
a new foundation had been prepared to Sarah's measurements.

Big Earl directed the trucks. Once Victoria's upper floor was hoisted into place,
they backed the lower floor underneath and let her down onto the concrete piers.

Sarah, Jess, and Mason stood looking at her after the movers left.

Mason yawned. "Home at last, Victoria."

As they drove away from the dark, disheveled house, Sarah waved. "See you tomorrow."

Day after day carpenters, plumbers, electricians, and painters swarmed over Victoria. Sarah came with drawings to see that the work was done right.

Two carpenters scabbed Victoria's studs back together again, while others leveled her gazebo.

Every day after school, Mason hurried over to watch the work. Willie, one of the carpenters, let Mason hand him nails as he repaired spindlework or put up wallboard in the attic.

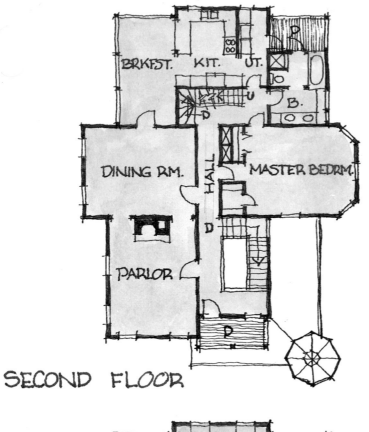

SECOND FLOOR

BRKFST. KIT. UT.

DINING RM.

HALL

MASTER BEDRM.

PARLOR

B.

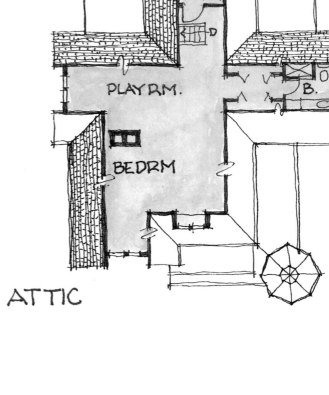

ATTIC

PLAY RM.

M.

B.

BEDRM

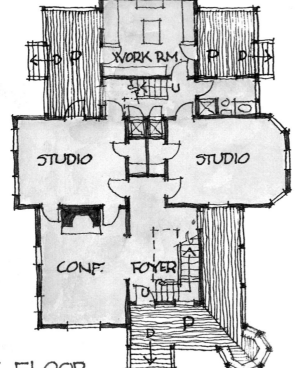

WORK RM.

STUDIO

STUDIO

CONF.

FOYER

FIRST FLOOR

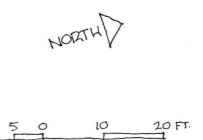

NORTH

BARNARD
PEARCE
AIA

10 5 0   10   20 FT.

SCALE

Workmen made the nursery into
a new kitchen upstairs where the family
would live and built a bathroom in the
attic. The downstairs was remodeled
into the new offices of Barnard-Pearce,
Architects. That was Jess and Sarah.

The painters used heat guns to
remove Victoria's old paint and rubbed
her down with sandpaper. They brushed
yellow paint on her siding and white
on her dainty trim.

Then one morning the moving van came. Sarah stood in the entry hall directing four men as they carried furniture and boxes into the house. Rugs were unrolled and each piece of furniture set in place. Mason bounded up and down the stairs to watch as the rooms came to life with tables and chairs, desks and beds, books and family photographs. Jess hung one of his oil paintings over the fireplace in the living room. Up in the attic, Mason opened a box marked *Beware of Snake*. He reached in and pulled out his long stuffed friend and coiled him on the window seat.

That evening lights went on all over Victoria. People came from up and down the
street to greet their new neighbors and to see the house that had been moved all the way
from the country. They brought bowls and platters of good food to eat, and even
a bucket of homemade ice cream. Big Earl and his boys came, and Willie, too.

As Mason lay in bed that night, he listened to Victoria's sounds. No longer were there creaks or groans. Talk and laughter drifted up from downstairs. Once again Victoria House was lived in and loved, and she sounded happy.